Sianne
the Butterfly
Fairy

Join the **Rainbow Magic Reading Challenge!**

Read the story and collect your fairy points to climb the

Rea~~~~~~~~~~~~~~~~~~~~~~~~~~~~~~

To all those who send wishes with the butterflies

Special thanks to
Rachel Elliot

ORCHARD BOOKS

First published in Great Britain in 2017 by The Watts Publishing Group

1 3 5 7 9 10 8 6 4 2

© 2017 Rainbow Magic Limited.
© 2017 HIT Entertainment Limited.
Illustrations © Orchard Books 2017

The moral rights of the author and illustrator have been asserted.

A CIP catalogue record for this book is available from the British Library.

ISBN 978 1 40835 168 0

Printed and bound in Great Britain by CPI Group (UK) Ltd, Croydon, CR0 4YY

The paper and board used in this book are made from wood from responsible sources

Orchard Books
An imprint of Hachette Children's Group
Part of The Watts Publishing Group Limited
Carmelite House, 50 Victoria Embankment, London EC4Y 0DZ

An Hachette UK Company
www.hachette.co.uk
www.hachettechildrens.co.uk

Sianne
the Butterfly
Fairy

by Daisy Meadows

ORCHARD

www.rainbowmagic.co.uk

Jack Frost's Spell

I want the fairies to be sad,
And human beings to feel bad.
When I control the butterflies,
I'll give them all a cold surprise.

With Sianne's magic in my hand,
I'll change the ways of Fairyland.
Humans will be full of fear,
And butterflies will disappear!

The Felt
Flower

Contents

Chapter One: A Special Surprise   11

Chapter Two: Magic in the Greenhouse   23

Chapter Three: The Butterfly Bridge   33

Chapter Four: Goblins on Guard   45

Chapter Five: A Clever Hiding Place   55

A Special Surprise

"Where are we going?" asked Kirsty Tate for the tenth time that morning.

Mrs Tate glanced at her in the rear-view mirror, and her eyes twinkled. Mr Tate turned around to look at his daughter.

"Haven't you guessed yet?" he asked, smiling.

The car slowed down and turned down
a narrow road. Kirsty bounced up and
down in her seat and gave a squeal of
excitement as she recognised the road.

"What is it?" asked her best friend,
Rachel Walker, who was sitting beside her.

"There's only one thing at the end of
this road," said Kirsty. "We're going to
the Wetherbury Butterfly Centre, right,
Mum? I've wanted to visit it ever since it
opened last year."

"I thought that it would be the perfect time to visit, while Rachel is here for the weekend," said Mrs Tate. "You two always seem to have so much fun when you're together."

Rachel and Kirsty exchanged a secret smile. Mrs Tate knew about some of the fun times they had together, but she had no idea about the secret they shared. When they were together, magical

adventures often seemed to follow them.

"Everyone says it's amazing there," Kirsty told Rachel. "There are lots of rare and exotic butterflies, and we can watch them coming out of chrysalises, and even go up in gliders to find out how it feels to fly."

Rachel couldn't help bouncing up and down as well.

"Oh, I've always wanted to go gliding," she said. "This is going to be an incredible day."

Mrs Tate pulled into the car park and found a space. Soon they were all walking into the foyer of the Butterfly Centre. Pictures of butterflies decorated the walls, and Rachel and Kirsty looked at the butterfly toys, books and pens on sale while Mr and Mrs Tate paid.

A young man was standing in front of some double doors with a small group of people. He had brown hair and a

cheerful, freckly face. He smiled when he saw them and beckoned them over.

"You're just in time to join our tour group," he said. "I'm Fred, and I'll be your guide today."

Rachel and Kirsty said hello to the group. There were three teenage friends, a family with two small children, and an elderly couple called Mr and Mrs Bird, as well as two young women called Carly and Jane. Everyone seemed to be friendly and excited about their visit.

"We're here to see if our grandchildren would like it," Mrs Bird explained. "They're coming to visit us soon."

"Would anyone like a carrot stick?" asked Carly.

"It's nice to see a young person eating

healthily," said Mr Bird.

"We like to take care of
our bodies," said Jane.

"We're training to be
professional football
players."

The teenagers, two
boys and a girl, looked
impressed.

"That's so cool," said
one of the boys. "Josh
here is a pretty good
football player himself."
He grinned at his
friend, who went pink
but looked pleased. Just then,
Fred cleared his throat and pushed open
the double doors.

"Welcome to the Wetherbury Butterfly

Centre," he said. "Please follow me."

He led them down a shadowy corridor, flickering with the rainbow colours of butterflies. Then they pushed through a thick plastic curtain, and found themselves in a huge greenhouse, filled with lush green plants and the sound of trickling water.

"It's like stepping into an oven," said Rachel.

Cameras and glasses were steaming

up. The girls blinked and gazed around.
Large, bright butterflies fluttered around
their heads, and Rachel and Kirsty gazed
up at them, delighted by each new colour
and pattern. Mr and Mrs Tate walked
over to a large plant with purple flowers.

The other people in the group moved around, examining the butterflies and plants.

"It reminds me of Fairyland," Kirsty whispered.

Magic in the Greenhouse

Rachel smiled at her best friend.
They had shared many adventures in
Fairyland, and it was full of beautiful
animals and plants, just like the Butterfly
Centre.

"The butterflies are most active on
warm, sunny days," Fred was saying.
"We have many different species

here. You'll see butterflies from South Africa, Thailand, Costa Rica and the Philippines."

"Look," Rachel whispered, hardly daring to breathe.

A large blue-and-yellow butterfly had landed on her hand. Kirsty didn't say anything, and when Rachel looked, she saw that a red-and-black butterfly had landed on her best friend's hand.

24

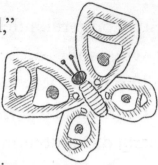

"They're so beautiful,"
Kirsty murmured.
At exactly the
same moment, the
two butterflies
rose into the air.

"See how they are
doing everything
together?" said
Rachel. "I wonder if
they are butterfly best
friends, just like us."

The butterflies fluttered
forwards a little way, and
then hovered.

"It's as if they're waiting for us," said
Kirsty.

"Let's follow them and see what
happens," said Rachel at once.

The butterflies flew ahead of them slowly, as if they wanted the girls to follow them. Rachel and Kirsty were led down a winding gravel path until they reached a little humpbacked bridge. The butterflies rested on the wooden handrail. It arched over a pond, and when the girls leaned over the rail they saw that the pond was full of shining goldfish.

As they were gazing down at the fish, a glowing butterfly flew out from under the bridge. It swooped up over their heads and then fluttered down to land on the handrail in front of them.

"That's not a butterfly," said Rachel in delight. "It's a fairy!"

The glimmering fairy was smiling up at Rachel and Kirsty. She was wearing a beautiful green dress decorated with little

butterflies, and a matching headband in the waves of her glossy blonde hair.

"Hello," she said.

"I'm Sianne the Butterfly Fairy."

"It's wonderful to meet you," said Kirsty. "I suppose you look after butterflies in the human world and in Fairyland?"

Sianne smiled.

"Not exactly," she said. "There is no difference between the butterflies in the two worlds. You see, butterflies are the only creatures that can travel between Fairyland and the human world. They have a very special job.

28

They carry wishes from your world to Fairyland, and they also carry messages between the fairies."

"I always thought that butterflies were kind of magical," said Rachel. "It sounds like I was right."

Sianne nodded. "I'm sorry to bother you in the middle of your special day," she went on, "but I've come to ask for your help."

"It makes any day more special to meet a fairy," said Rachel.

"We are always happy to help our fairy friends however we can," Kirsty added.

"What's happened?"

"It's Jack Frost," said Sianne. "He's been extra grumpy with the fairies lately, because the way he sees it, we keep stopping him from doing exactly what he wants. He came up with an especially mean plan to get his revenge. He knows how much we care about humans, so he decided to spoil the butterfly connection between the fairy and human worlds. He has stolen my magical objects so that he can control the butterflies."

Rachel and Kirsty exchanged a horrified glance.

"What do your magical objects do?"
Rachel asked.

"They are special because they help
both butterflies and human beings," said
Sianne. "The felt flower helps butterflies
and people be strong at difficult times.
The crystal chrysalis helps butterflies
transform and people be the best they
can be. The silver wings help butterflies
fly and people achieve their dreams."

"What has Jack Frost done with them?"
said Kirsty.

"I don't know," said Sianne. "But he
has trapped some of the butterflies in
a guarded glass house outside the Ice
Castle, and he has said that he won't let
them carry human wishes to the fairies
ever again."

The Butterfly Bridge

"We'll do everything we can to help," Kirsty promised. "It would be a terrible thing to leave the human world without wishes."

Rachel was gazing up and frowning. "How strange," she said suddenly.

Kirsty looked up too, and saw something unusual. Several butterflies were flying in single file, copying each other exactly. They were swooping and fluttering as if they were playing Follow My Leader.

"They have been called to Fairyland by my magic," said Sianne. "Nothing can stop them from going to Jack Frost."

"Maybe we should follow them," said Rachel. "This might be our chance to get the magical objects back."

Rachel and Kirsty still had their hands resting on the wooden handrail of the humpbacked bridge. Sianne gently tapped their little fingers with her wand, and a ripple of rainbow-coloured light flickered across their hands, up their arms and all over their bodies. They blinked as fairy dust dazzled them, and then they were fluttering beside Sianne on tiny gossamer wings, no bigger than the butterflies.

"We're fairies again," said Rachel, pirouetting in mid-air. "I love the feeling of my wings lifting me upwards."

"Let's follow the butterflies," said Kirsty.

The fairies swooped after the butterflies. They zoomed up to the roof of the butterfly house and

saw Kirsty's parents far below.

"Time will stand still until we return from Fairyland," said Sianne. "They won't even know you've gone."

The butterflies dived swiftly down and disappeared under the humpbacked bridge. The fairies followed, and there was a bright flash of golden light. Then they were fluttering across the blue sky of Fairyland.

"That took my breath away," said Rachel.

"There are

not many secret gateways to Fairyland from the human world," said Sianne. "The humpbacked bridge is one of them."

"Where have the butterflies gone?" asked Kirsty, scanning the skyline.

"I can't see any butterflies, but I can see some old friends," said Rachel, breaking into a big smile.

Sienna the Saturday Fairy and Sarah the Sunday Fairy were zooming towards them, waving. They hugged Sianne.

"We've been watching over you two," said Sarah to Rachel and Kirsty. "We wanted to make sure that you have the perfect weekend together. We had no idea we'd get the chance to say hello here in Fairyland!"

"That's so kind of you," said Kirsty.

"Have you seen any butterflies nearby?" asked Sianne.

"Yes, we've just seen lots of them heading in the direction of the Ice Castle," said Sienna. "We wondered if we would see you, Sianne. Is Jack Frost up to no good as usual?"

Sianne nodded, and Sarah and Sienna smiled at Rachel and Kirsty.

"It looks as if you have the very best help," said Sarah. "Rachel and Kirsty are the most wonderful friends of Fairyland. But please, if you need us, just call."

"Thank you," said Sianne. "We have to follow the butterflies now, but hopefully this will soon be over and I can come and tell you all about it."

They waved goodbye to Sienna and Sarah, and zoomed towards the Ice Castle. Soon they were flying above the garden. A brand-new building had appeared there – an arched glass house made from lots of hexagonal panes. Around the building, all the flowerbeds were in full bloom.

"That's strange," said Rachel. "Usually

Jack Frost's flowerbeds are filled with bare
bushes and weeds."

But they forgot all about the flowers
when they hovered above the glass house
and looked down. There were many
butterflies sitting inside, their wings

drooping on the floor. Not a single one was fluttering in the air. Several goblins guarded the door.

"My poor butterflies look scared," said Sianne. "Something is very wrong. Butterflies are normally strong

and brave. They never stop trying to escape if they are trapped."

"Why are they staying on the ground in there?" Kirsty asked.

"It's because the felt flower is missing," said Sianne. "Without it, the butterflies can't be strong and brave and they won't be able to carry out their special job. Oh, I can't bear it! We have to set them free right now."

43

Goblins on Guard

"Wait," said Rachel. "Look at all the goblin guards. The butterflies won't have the courage to try to escape past them without the felt flower. We must find it."

"Where could Jack Frost be keeping it?" said Kirsty. "We should search the castle – it must be in there somewhere."

"But how can we get in?" asked Sianne.
Rachel smiled.

"Leave that to us," she said. "We've
been here many times, and we've found
a few hidden entrances and secret ways
in. I'm sure we'll be able to creep in
somewhere."

They led Sianne towards the castle,
remembering the many magical
adventures that had led them here before.

"Let's try the trapdoor on the roof," said
Rachel.

They fluttered over the battlements, but
to their disappointment they saw two
goblins sitting on top of the trapdoor. The
goblins waved at them and grinned.

"No luck here," they called out in sing-
song voices.

"Oh no, we've been spotted," said
Sianne.

They flew over the courtyard, hoping

to swoop down there if it was empty, but they soon had another disappointment. Goblins sat at every corner, playing card games and squabbling. They all sniggered when they looked up and saw the fairies.

"Why aren't they more worried by seeing us?" asked Kirsty. "There's something strange about this."

The fairies flew on, checking doorways,

windows and secret entrances. Every

single one was
locked and guarded.
Goblins capered
around inside
the castle, pulling
faces at them from
the windows and
laughing as the

fairies kept searching for a way in.

They flew past the main entrance, and
one of the goblin guards looked up and
spotted
them. He
nudged
the goblins
beside him,
and they all
pointed and

squawked with laughter.

"You'll never get your things back," they shouted at Sianne. "Jack Frost is one step ahead of you."

When they flew past the Throne Room window, they heard a mean voice calling out to them.

"Coo-ee," said Jack Frost.

He was leaning out of the window, resting his elbows on the windowsill and scowling at them. As they watched, he raised one hand and

waggled his fingers in a nasty wave.

"Come in and search wherever you like," he said with a smug smile. "You will never find it. A whole pack of silly fairies wouldn't be clever enough to figure out my hiding place."

Kirsty stopped flying so suddenly that Sianne and Rachel bumped into her. She turned and faced them, hovering in mid-air.

"I have a bad feeling that Jack Frost is a step ahead of us for once," she said. "I would expect him to be more worried that we're here, and ordering the goblins to catch us."

"It's as if we're doing exactly what they want us to do," said Rachel.

"If Jack Frost is being clever, we have to be even cleverer," Kirsty said.

"What do you mean?" asked Sianne.

"He wants us to search the castle for your felt flower, so he probably hasn't hidden it in the castle at all," said Kirsty.

"Yes, he must be trying to trap us," said Rachel. "Come on, surely we can outsmart Jack Frost and his goblins. We have to try to work out where he would have hidden the felt flower. We have to think like Jack Frost."

A Clever Hiding Place

"I'm not sure I can think like Jack Frost," said Rachel. "But I have an idea. I once read a story which said the best place to hide something was among lots of other similar things."

"What do you mean?" asked Sianne.

"Like a tree in a forest, or a needle in

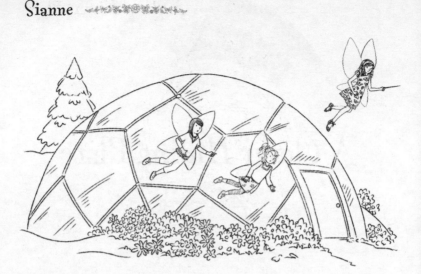

a sewing basket," said Rachel. "Or ... a flower in a flowerbed!"

"Of course," said Kirsty. "Good thinking, Rachel. I bet that's exactly where he's hidden it. We have to get back to the garden as fast as we can!"

In a flash, the fairies were speeding towards the Ice Castle garden again. The flowers around the butterfly house seemed even more beautiful than before. Blooms of every size and colour nodded

and waved in flowerbed after flowerbed.

"We'll have to split up and search," said Rachel.

As they swooped low over the flowers, they heard Jack Frost yelling at them from the castle. Looking back, they saw him leaning out of a high window, shaking his fist. He didn't look smug any more.

"Get away from my flowers, you interfering pests!" he bellowed.

"Now we know that we're on the right track," said Kirsty. "The felt flower is here somewhere."

"Hurry," Sianne called. "If he reaches us before we find it, we'll lose our chance to save the butterflies."

"What does it look like?" Rachel asked.

"You'll know it when you see it," Sianne assured her.

Rachel, Kirsty and Sianne skimmed over the flowerbeds, so low that the pollen dust brushed against their clothes. They scanned left and right, trying not to miss a single petal in their search. Then an angry shout jolted through them like an electric shock.

"Get away!" Jack Frost shrieked. "I'll drop you in my dungeon! I'll lock you under my lake!"

He was running out of the castle towards them, his cloak flapping behind him like the wings of an angry bird.

"He's coming!" Sianne cried.

They flew on and on, faster and faster. Rachel and Kirsty were panting, the cold air hurting their lungs. They felt as if they couldn't go on, but they would not give up. Sianne was depending on them.

Suddenly, Kirsty saw a flower that glimmered as if it were made of diamonds. She swooped closer and saw that it had been sprinkled with fairy dust.

"I think I've found it!" she cried out.

Sianne zoomed towards her, and Jack Frost let out a furious wail. But he was still several strides away, too far to throw

himself between Kirsty and the flower.
She put out her hand to the glittering
flower, and it seemed to jump into her
hand. Now she could feel that it was
made of felt, and her heart gave a leap of
happiness. They had done it!

Kirsty handed the flower to Sianne.
Instantly, the butterflies inside the glass

house swirled into the air. In a glorious
whirl of colour, they hurled themselves

towards the door. The goblin guards
turned and squealed.

"I don't like it!" one of them wailed.
"Too many flappy wings!"

"Let's get out of here," said another.

They ran off, and Sianne opened the door with a wave of her wand.

"You're free," she called out to the butterflies. "Go and take the humans' wishes to the fairies."

Soaring and tumbling through the air like flying flowers, the butterflies went in all directions. Sianne turned to Rachel and Kirsty with a smile.

"Thank you with all my heart," she said. "It was wonderful to be able to save those butterflies. I will send you back to the Butterfly Centre now, but I will see you again very soon."

"Promise?" said Rachel.

Sianne smiled.

"I promise," she said.

The Crystal
Chrysalis

Contents

Chapter Six: The Butterfly Nursery   69

Chapter Seven: Caterpillar Quiz   77

Chapter Eight: Chrysalis Crisis   87

Chapter Nine: Goblin Games   97

Chapter Ten: The Third Bag   107

The Butterfly Nursery

Rachel and Kirsty felt a wave of heat wash over them. They were back on the humpbacked bridge in the middle of the Butterfly Centre.

"Come on, let's go and find Mum and Dad," said Kirsty, running off the bridge.

Rachel followed her, and they ran back down the winding gravel path to the place where they had left their tour group. Mr and Mrs Tate were still looking at the same plant.

"No time has passed at all while we've been in Fairyland," whispered Rachel.

Fred called the tour group together.

"Please follow me to the butterfly nursery," he said. "This is one of the most magical places in the centre. Here you will see where the chrysalises hang until the butterflies emerge."

He led everyone into a separate chamber, where dozens of chrysalises were hanging on the walls.

"There are so many different colours and sizes," said Carly in surprise.

"Yes, as many as there are different butterflies," said Fred. "There are lots

of different species, but they all share the same life cycle. First, an egg is attached to the leaf or stem of a plant. A caterpillar is born, and its job is to eat lots and grow fast."

"What do they eat?" asked one of the other children in the group.

"A caterpillar eats the leaves of plants and trees," said Fred. "It grows to fill its skin, but the skin doesn't stretch. So a caterpillar has to shed its skin four or five times because it grows so much and so fast. When the caterpillar reaches the end of its life, it finds a special place and sheds its skin for the last time."

"Is that when it becomes a chrysalis?" asked Jane.

Fred nodded. "Inside the chrysalis, the caterpillar changes into its adult shape. It doesn't move, eat or drink," he said.

One of the teenage boys that the girls had met earlier nudged his friend Josh.

"It sounds as lazy as you," he said in a mean voice.

Rachel and Kirsty exchanged a look of surprise.

"They seemed like really good friends earlier," said Rachel in a low voice. "Maybe they've fallen out."

The boys were still bickering, and the teenage girl suddenly stamped her foot.

"Shut up, both of you," she snapped. "I'm trying to listen."

"Soon you should see some butterflies coming out of the chrysalises," said Fred. "The best time to see them is between ten o'clock in the morning and one o'clock in the afternoon."

"What do the butterflies eat?" Mrs Bird asked.

"Most of them feed on nectar, which they collect from flowers," said Fred. "They have a long, hollow tube called a proboscis, and they suck the nectar up through that, the same way that you might suck a drink through a straw. As you walk around the butterfly farm, you might see rotting fruit lying here and there. That's because some butterflies enjoy feeding on it."

"Yuck, that sounds disgusting," said Jane, curling her lip.

Fred gave a nervous smile, and Rachel and Kirsty felt sorry for him.

"OK, while you're waiting for the first chrysalis to open, we have a few quiz questions for you," he said. "It's a way to see how much you already know about butterflies. Choose one of the screens and press the start button."

Caterpillar Quiz

Fred waved his hand towards several computer screens dotted around the walls of the butterfly nursery. Rachel and Kirsty went over to the nearest screen, where Josh and his friends were already standing. Josh pressed the start button and a computerised voice spoke.

"Welcome to the butterfly quiz," it said.

"Question one. What does a caterpillar do when it gets too big for its skin?"

Josh looked at his friends. They all shrugged.

"Fred just told us this," said Kirsty, trying to remind them. "It's a bit like ... like taking off a coat."

She waited, but the others looked at their feet, refusing to catch her eye.

"You know this," said Rachel.

"I don't want to get it wrong," muttered Josh. "It'd be terrible to fail."

"The only way to fail is to stop trying," said Kirsty.

But Josh and his friends shook their heads and trudged away from the monitor. Rachel and Kirsty went to follow the teenagers, and bumped straight into Carly and Jane. They were huddled together, sharing a bag of chips and munching on two greasy hamburgers.

"Forget about carrot sticks, these are way more yummy," they heard Carly say.

Mr and Mrs Bird were walking out of the butterfly nursery, and Fred called out to them as they reached the door.

"It won't be long till the chrysalises open," he said. "If you just wait a little longer ..."

"We haven't got the time for this nonsense," Mr Bird snapped. "Our grandchildren probably wouldn't like it here anyway."

"They'd just be rude and ungrateful," added Mrs Bird in a cross voice. "Just like all children are nowadays – badly behaved."

Mr and Mrs Bird left the butterfly nursery, and Rachel pulled Kirsty to one side.

"I think I know why everyone is being so horrible," she said in a low voice. "It's because Sianne's crystal chrysalis is missing. Without it, people aren't being the best they can be.

They're being the worst."

"I'm sure you're right," Kirsty said. "I hope Sianne comes back soon so that we can help her to find it. Look – more people are leaving."

Two strangely dressed people were slipping out of the door. One was wearing an enormous hat draped in

feathers that hid her face. The other had a scarf pulled up over his nose and a cap tugged down over his head.

"I don't remember them being part of our tour group," said Rachel.

"But there *is* something about them that I recognise," said Kirsty.

As the second person left the nursery, his scarf dropped down and Rachel glimpsed a long, green nose, covered in warts. She grabbed Kirsty's arm and made

her jump.

"Goblins," she whispered. "Kirsty, they're goblins!"

The girls glanced at Mr and Mrs Tate, and saw that they were looking in the opposite direction. Quickly, Rachel and Kirsty hurried out of the nursery and

back into the main greenhouse. There
were a couple of other tour groups
wandering around, but the goblins had
disappeared.

"Let's go back towards the bridge," said
Kirsty. "Maybe we can ask a butterfly to
take a message to Sianne."

Chrysalis Crisis

The girls hurried down the path and stopped in the middle of the humpbacked bridge. At once, a large red butterfly started to flutter around them. They waited for a couple of families to pass by,

and then
Kirsty lifted
her hands
into the air.
The red
butterfly
landed on
her index
finger.

"Please take a message to Sianne for us," said Kirsty. "It's urgent. Tell her that we have seen goblins in the Butterfly Centre."

"There's no need to send a butterfly message," said a familiar voice.

The girls looked up and saw Sianne perching on a branch above them. She smiled and flicked her wand. Silver fairy dust shot out from the tip, bounced down

on to the
wooden
bridge and
surrounded
them in a
glittering
cloud.

"It's
like being
wrapped up in tinsel," said Kirsty in
delight.

Seconds later, they were sitting on the
branch beside Sianne, fluttering their
wings.

"So you saw goblins here?" Sianne
asked.

"They were in disguise," said Rachel.
"We followed them out of the butterfly
nursery, but they disappeared."

"What could they be doing here?" Kirsty asked.

"Causing mischief," said Sianne. "Jack Frost is still trying to use my magical objects to harm the butterflies. We must find the goblins. Whatever they're doing, you can be sure it's not good."

"Let's fly close to the roof and search for them," said Rachel.

The fairies rose into the air and flew up until their wings fluttered against

the glass ceiling. Then they began to fly over the plants and trees, scanning the greenhouse for the goblins.

"Everyone has been behaving strangely," Kirsty told Sianne. "People are losing their patience. They don't seem to care about doing their best or trying their hardest."

"Is it because the crystal chrysalis is missing?" Rachel asked. "You said that it helps people to be the best they can be."

"Yes," said Sianne, looking serious. "But

the crystal chrysalis doesn't only help people to be the best they can be."

She pointed down to where Fred was talking anxiously to another tour guide.

The fairies fluttered closer and crouched down behind a yellow tropical flower.

"Not a single one has opened yet," Fred

was saying. "It's almost twelve o'clock. Usually lots of them have opened by now. Something's wrong."

"But what can we do about it?" the

other tour guide asked him, shrugging her shoulders. "We just have to blame Mother Nature."

"It's got nothing to do with Mother Nature, and everything to do with Jack Frost," said Sianne quietly. "The crystal chrysalis helps butterflies to transform, too. While Jack Frost has it, no new butterflies can be born. We have to get it back."

Fred and the tour guide walked away, and Sianne stood up.

"I want to go and see the chrysalises," she said. "They might not be able to hear me, but I'd like to tell them that we're working hard to keep them safe."

"We'll come with you," said Rachel. "But we have to be careful. There are a lot of people around, and we mustn't be seen."

Flying close to the plants and flowers, the fairies made their way towards the butterfly nursery. The tour group had left, but there were two people still in the room.

"That's them," said Kirsty. "Those are the goblins."

Goblin Games

The goblins were poking at the rows of brown and green chrysalises that were hanging on the wall. Then they started to pull the chrysalises down and shove them into two green velvet pouches.

"Jack Frost is still trying to take all the butterflies," said Sianne. "We can't allow this. The chrysalises are helpless, and it's my job to keep them safe."

Rachel put her arm around Sianne's shoulders and gave her a comforting hug.

"Our job," she said.

Kirsty took Sianne's hand.

"We won't stop trying until we have all your magical objects," she said.

"Thank you," said Sianne. "But how are we going to stop the goblins? They're so much bigger than we are."

"There's no need to be scared of someone just because they're bigger," said Rachel in a determined voice. "We can stop them by being cleverer than they are."

Together, the fairies flew between the goblins and the chrysalises.

"Stop!" said Kirsty.

"You must not steal these chrysalises,"

said Sianne, tilting her chin up a little. "We will not allow it."

The goblins laughed at them, and then the one in the hat started juggling with three green bags, throwing them higher and higher into the air.

"You can't stop us, you silly little fairies," he said, cackling. "Oh dear, what sad faces. Are you feeling worried about these little bags? Shall we see if we can get them any higher?"

He threw the bags to the other goblin

and they giggled as they flung them across the room.

"Stop!" cried Sianne. "You might hurt the chrysalises!"

"I've got an idea," whispered Kirsty. "What if you were to make lots of the same green bags? If Rachel and I juggle too, we might be able to confuse the goblins and rescue the chrysalises."

Sianne's eyes sparkled.

"This could work," she said, raising her wand.

"*The goblins here are acting tough,*

So two green bags are not enough.

*Return my friends to human form
So they can juggle and perform."*
There was a magical flash of light, and
Rachel and Kirsty were human again,
their hands full of green velvet pouches.
At once, they started to juggle.

"Hey, what's going on?" cried the
goblins in confusion.

Rachel threw one of her pouches to the goblin with the feathery hat and he

caught it. "Stop that!" he snapped, and she threw another one.

Kirsty threw one too, and soon all the pouches were flying through the air. The goblins started to giggle and throw the pouches back at them. Every time the girls caught a new pouch, they peeped inside. The ones that Sianne had made were empty, but after a few moments,

Rachel opened one that contained chrysalises.

"Got one," she whispered to Kirsty. "Keep looking."

After checking five more bags, Kirsty found the other chrysalises. At once, they stopped throwing the bags.

"Sianne, the chrysalises are safe," said Rachel.

The girls hurried over to the little fairy and held up the bags. With a wave of her wand, Sianne returned the chrysalises to the wall.

"Hey, that's not fair," the goblin with the cap shouted, pulling the scarf down from his mouth. "You're spoiling our game."

"Stealing chrysalises is not a game," said Sianne in a stern voice.

"Hang on a minute," said Rachel. "A minute ago the goblin had three bags, not two. What was in the third bag?"

The Third Bag

The goblins exchanged a horrified look, and Rachel and Kirsty guessed the answer at exactly the same time.

"They've got the crystal chrysalis," said Kirsty.

"And it's in one of these bags," Rachel added, gazing at the velvet pouches piled on the floor.

"Leave them alone," squawked the goblin with the feathery hat. "That shiny thing belongs to Jack Frost now."

"That's nonsense," said Sianne. "Rachel, Kirsty, we have to find it before they can take it back to Jack Frost."

Rachel, Kirsty and the two goblins dived into the piles of velvet bags. In a panic, the goblins tore open the pouches. The girls opened one after another, trying to stay calm. Sianne fluttered anxiously between them, watching their fingers work faster and faster. She crossed her fingers for luck.

"Got it!" cried Kirsty.

She jumped up, holding a green pouch in her hand. The goblins flung themselves across the room at her, and she threw

the pouch into the air. A small, shining chrysalis was flung up, catching the light as it turned over and over. Sianne zoomed after it, and it fell into her outstretched arms. Instantly, it shrank to fairy size.

The two goblins turned on each other. "You'll be in trouble when Jack Frost hears about this!" squealed the goblin with the feathery hat.

"You're the one who had the pouch," the other goblin retorted. "He'll have you scrubbing the dungeons for this."

"He'll make you sweep up the snow."

"He'll turn you into a gargoyle."

"He'll make you into goblin gruel."

"Dimwit!"

"Fool!"

"Please stop arguing," said Rachel.

111

The goblins stopped shouting and turned to glare at her.

"Jack Frost still has the silver wings," said the goblin with the cap. "Even if he can't own all the butterflies, he'll never let them do their job again."

The goblins turned and scurried out of the butterfly nursery, pushing and shoving each other as they went. Their voices faded into the distance.

"Thank you," said Sianne, fluttering between the girls. "Once again you have saved one of my magical objects, and you have helped save the butterflies."

"We were glad to do it," said Kirsty. "Are you going to take the crystal chrysalis back home now?"

Sianne nodded.

"I will go through the secret gateway under the bridge," said Sianne. "Will you come and wave goodbye?"

"Of course," said the girls.

Sianne flew into the pocket of Kirsty's trousers, and the girls ran down the path to the humpbacked bridge. As soon as there was no one else around, Sianne flew out and waved to

Rachel and Kirsty. Then she dived under the bridge, and with a little puff of fairy dust, she was gone. The sparkling powder sparkled on the surface of the pond for a moment, and the goldfish looked up at it in surprise.

"Kirsty, Rachel, where are you?" called Mrs Tate from the other side of

the greenhouse. "Come quickly – the chrysalises are opening!"

The girls ran to join her. Inside the butterfly nursery, Fred's tour group had returned. Mr and Mrs Bird were watching the chrysalises, looking excited. Josh and his friends were laughing together, and Carly and Jane were eating celery sticks.

"It looks as if they're all back to normal," Rachel said in a low voice.

"Come and see, girls," Mr Tate called to them. "It's amazing."

They gathered in front of the chrysalises with the rest of the group, and watched as one of them started to twitch. It was almost see-through, and it broke apart easily as the butterfly inside pushed and stretched. Clinging to the chrysalis, it dangled and slowly unfolded its crumpled yellow wings. Everyone stood in wonder and silence, watching until the wings looked strong and smooth, and the butterfly rose into the air.

"That was incredible," said Rachel.

"And we've found out that there's magic in the human world too," said Kirsty with a smile. "A brand-new butterfly opening its wings!"

116

The Silver Wings

Contents

Chapter Eleven: Sunny's Dream   121

Chapter Twelve: Sianne's Fairyland Home   133

Chapter Thirteen: Jack Frost's Plan   145

Chapter Fourteen: Frosty Fluff Pot   155

Chapter Fifteen: A Dream Come True   165

Sunny's Dream

When Rachel and Kirsty left the greenhouse, the air outside seemed cold, even though it was a warm, sunny day. They gazed at the rolling hills around the Butterfly Centre.

"This has been such an exciting day," said Rachel to Mr and Mrs Tate. "Thank you for inviting me along."

"It's not over yet," said Mrs Tate with a smile. "You two have a glider flight to get ready for."

The girls exchanged a thrilled glance. "In all the excitement with Sianne, I forgot about the glider flight," Kirsty whispered. "I wonder what it'll be like to fly as human beings."

"Flying
without wings,
and without
being fairy-
sized," said
Rachel. "It will
be strange."
Fred was
behind them,
and he handed

some paperwork to Mrs Tate.

"Take the girls up to the hilltop
glider station ahead," he said. "Give the
instructors the paperwork and they will
show you what to do."

The Tates and Rachel made their way
up the buttercup-covered hill to the little
glider station at the top. The instructors
were out with other visitors, but there

was one family waiting inside the little station — a mother, a father and a little girl in a wheelchair.

"Hi," said Rachel, smiling at her. "I'm Rachel, and this is my best Kirsty. Are you here for a glider ride too?"

The girl smiled. "Hi, I'm Sunny," she said. "I can hardly wait for the glider ride. It's going to be the biggest adventure I've ever had. I've dreamed all my life of being able to fly. Have you two ever flown before?"

Rachel and Kirsty exchanged a quick smile.

"Not like this," said Rachel.

Just then, the two instructors came into the station.

"Welcome," said the first. "I'm Harry and this is Meg. We'll be helping you find

out how it feels to fly like the butterflies today. We just have to check over our equipment first."

"Is something wrong?" asked Kirsty. "Why do you need to check it if you were just using it?"

"We have to be super safe," said Meg with a smile. "Don't worry – there's

nothing wrong. It's our usual safety check."

Rachel, Kirsty and Sunny watched as Harry and Meg laid out their equipment.

"Hang on, I've got a rope tangle here," said Meg.

There was a long wait while the rope was untangled. Then Harry found a

broken clip and had to search for a
replacement.

"Isn't that a rip in your glider wing?"
asked Mr Tate,
pointing.

Harry and
Meg groaned,
and Sunny
hung her head.

"This isn't
going to
happen, is it?"
she said to
Rachel and
Kirsty. "I should have known that dreams
don't really come true."

"It looks as if they're having problems
down at the Butterfly Centre too," said
Meg suddenly.

Below, they saw
Fred hurrying
out of the centre
and coming up
towards them. He
shook his head
when he heard
that the gliders
were having
problems.

"Everything's
going wrong
today," he said. "I was coming up to say
that we might have to close the whole
centre. All the butterflies have stopped
flying. Not a single one is rising into the
air or fluttering around the plants."

"At this rate, no one's going to be
flying today," said Harry.

Just then, Kirsty saw something move out of the corner of her eye. She nudged Rachel, and together they edged over to the entrance. When they peeped around the corner, they saw Sianne hovering in front of them.

"Be careful," said Rachel. "If anyone comes out of the Butterfly Centre, they'll see you at once."

"Then please come with me straight away," said Sianne, wringing her hands together. "Jack Frost has let his goblins loose on my home, and I need your help. We have to get the goblins out of there!"

Sianne's Fairyland Home

With a single wave of Sianne's wand, the girls were standing in Fairyland with pastel-coloured wings fluttering behind them.

"I'm sorry I had to whisk you here so

suddenly," said Sianne. "But look!"

She waved her arm towards a large house. It was unlike anything the girls had seen before, in Fairyland or the human world. The building was shaped like butterfly wings, and the front was made entirely of glass. The glass swirled with faint hues of rose, lilac and yellow, and sweet-smelling purple butterfly bushes surrounded it, dotted with blooms.

"What beautiful flowers," said Kirsty.

"Usually, butterflies from all around the world flutter in and out of the flowers," said Sianne. "But today, their wings are still. They are just sitting on the flowers and plants, unable to move – even though there are goblins inside my home."

Among the flowers were large, beautiful butterflies in every colour of the rainbow.

It was a magical sight, but Sianne was looking sad.

"As long as the silver wings are missing, the butterflies will not be able to lift off the ground," she went on. "Jack Frost will have succeeded, and butterflies will not be able to carry the wishes of human beings. The only hope is if we can do something

to stop him right now."
Rachel and Kirsty
looked at each other
and nodded.

"We'll do everything
we can," Rachel
promised. "Show us
where the goblins are
– first we need to try
to get them to leave."
Sianne zoomed
forward and Rachel
and Kirsty followed
close behind. There was a small door in
the centre of the glass front of the house.

"Usually it opens at my touch," said
Sianne. "But look."

She gently pressed her hand against the
door, but it stayed firmly shut.

"I think it needs some helping hands," said Kirsty.

She and Rachel pressed their hands against the glass door beside Sianne's, and pushed with all their strength. Slowly, the glass door opened. As soon as the crack was wide enough to let them through, they squeezed in to the house.

The first thing that struck them was the noise. The cackles and squawks of goblins

echoed all around
them, bouncing off
the glass
walls and
ceiling
and making
their heads
ring. It
was hard
to know
which way to turn – the noise seemed to
be coming from all directions at once.

Like the greenhouse in Wetherbury,
Sianne's house was very hot and very
light. Beautiful plants intertwined from
floor to ceiling, and all the rooms were
open to each other, so the whole house
was a tangle of branches, vines and
blooms. Delicate woodland pictures

were painted on the floor. Chrysalises hung from twigs and stems – and so did a crowd of goblins. Shouting, shrieking and squawking, they swung from the branches and dangled from the vines. They were throwing bags of flour and eggs at each other, and usually missing, so the whole house was coated in a thin layer of white powder and dripping raw egg.

"My home is

usually a calm place," said Sianne, deeply upset. "They have turned it into a loud, messy goblin playground."

"They must be made to leave!" cried Rachel, feeling hurt and shocked for Sianne. "You naughty goblins, get out of here! You're going to scare the butterflies." Rachel, Kirsty and Sianne flew up

and down the house, trying to shoo the goblins away. They flew together and then separately, but the goblins still zigzagged out of their reach. They tried picking up the goblins one by one and carrying them outside, but they just sneaked back in. Panting and feeling helpless, the three fairies hovered in the middle of the house.

"What now?" asked Sianne. "We can't give up, but nothing seems to be working. The goblins have us flying around in circles."

"Oh," said Kirsty suddenly. "Of course!"

"What is it?" Rachel asked.

"I think I know what the goblins are doing," said Kirsty. "Jack Frost has made them cause trouble like this before – but only when he wanted to distract us from his real plan. He wants us to spend time chasing the goblins, because he's doing something else – something that he doesn't want us to notice."

"What do you think he's doing?" asked
Sianne.

"What are the most important things in
your home?" asked Kirsty quickly.

"My most important things are my
magical objects," said Sianne. "But we
already have two of them back. Jack Frost
couldn't be planning to steal them for a
second time ... could he?"

Jack Frost's Plan

The fairies looked at each other and a feeling of dread crept over them.

"It would be very clever," said Rachel. "He would know that we wouldn't be expecting it."

Without another word, Sianne zoomed

down to the painted
woodland scene on
the floor of her house.
Among the painted
green leaves was
a picture of a
red admiral
butterfly, and
now Sianne
pointed

her wand directly at it. To the girls'
amazement, the picture began to move.
The painted wings trembled and lifted, to
reveal a set of stone steps leading down
underneath the house.

"A secret passageway," said Rachel in a
breathless voice. "That's so clever, Sianne."

"Follow me," said the Butterfly Fairy.
She hurried down the steps into the

darkness, and Rachel and Kirsty were
close behind her. The steps spiralled deep
down into underground caves, and the
noise of the goblins faded to a distant

hum. As the
light faded,
Sianne held
up her wand,
and the tip
lit up like
a glowing
torch.

At the
bottom of
the steps, the
three fairies
stopped
in front of
an arched

wooden door.

"We'll go in together on the count of three," Sianne whispered. "One ... two ... three!"

They flung the door open and saw Jack Frost leaning over a glass table. The felt flower and the crystal chrysalis were lying on top of it. Without stopping to think, Rachel and Kirsty darted forwards and hovered between the Ice Lord and Sianne's magical objects.

"Interfering pests!" Jack Frost said with a scowl. "Out of my way! Those things are mine – I put in a lot of work to steal them."

"Never," said Kirsty, linking arms with Rachel. Sianne joined them.

Jack Frost raised his wand.

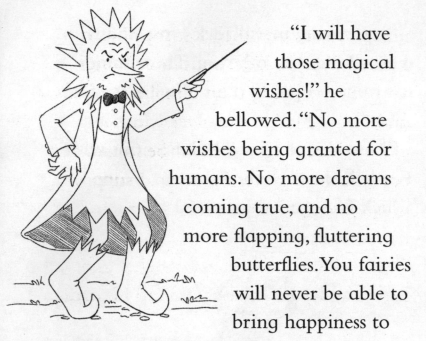

"I will have those magical wishes!" he bellowed. "No more wishes being granted for humans. No more dreams coming true, and no more flapping, fluttering butterflies. You fairies will never be able to bring happiness to the human world again, and my revenge will be complete!"

"Give back the silver wings," Rachel insisted. "Sianne has got her other objects back, and we won't allow you to take them a second time. You have lost."

"You will never get the silver wings," Jack Frost said, sneering. "My goblins are

nincompoops and they lost the objects
I asked them to hide, but I am cleverer
and more cunning than a million goblins,
and I have hidden the silver wings in a
place where they will never be found. The
butterflies will never fly again. I suppose
you're going to have to change their
name! Ha!"

Jack Frost tried to shove Rachel and
Kirsty aside, but they held on to his arms.

Sianne waved her wand, and the felt flower and the crystal chrysalis flew into her hands. Jack Frost bared his teeth and

shook Rachel and Kirsty off. Then he flicked his wand, and a small storm cloud appeared, flashing with blue lightning. Jack Frost stepped on to it.

"Take me away from these flimsy fairies!" he commanded.

"We have to follow him," Rachel whispered to Kirsty. "If we lose him now, we might never find out where he's hidden the silver wings."

There was no time to tell Sianne what they were doing. Together, the best friends grabbed hold of the edge of the cloud, and they were yanked away from Sianne's home in the blink of an eye.

Frosty Fluff Pot

Rachel and Kirsty clung to the cloud
with all their strength. It felt a bit like
trying to hold on to wet cotton wool.
They were hurtling through the air so fast
that they could hardly breathe. The grey

storm cloud dragged them faster than they had ever flown, their hair and wings streaming out behind them.

In a blur, they saw the green hills of Fairyland below them, followed by the darker corner where the Ice Castle and Goblin Grotto stood. Then the scene below turned white, and they were zooming over the high ice mountains. The cloud began to slow down, and Rachel and Kirsty saw frozen glaciers and jagged, snowy peaks. Then they felt themselves sinking towards the highest of the icy mountains.

"Quick," Kirsty whispered. "Let's hide on the mountaintop and watch what he does."

Staying behind Jack Frost, the best friends fluttered down and crouched behind a large boulder that was glittering with frost. They watched Jack Frost step off his storm cloud and jump into the powdery snow.

"He hasn't spotted us," said Rachel in a low voice.

Her breath hung mistily in the air as they watched Jack Frost raise one of his long, spindly legs. Then he stamped on the mountaintop three times. There was a loud groaning sound, and then Rachel and Kirsty saw a large boulder give a little twitch. The snow was jerked off it. The boulder shook again, and then rolled slowly to the feet of the Ice Lord. There was a loud crack,

and the boulder opened like an egg. A
bright light shone out of it, and at first it
dazzled Rachel and Kirsty. They blinked,
and then saw a delicate silver model of
butterfly wings.

"We've found it," Kirsty whispered,
squeezing Rachel's hand in excitement.

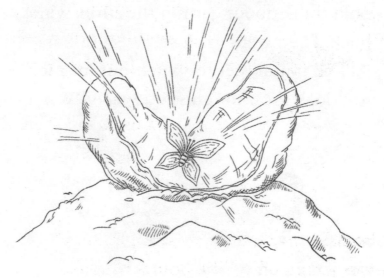

Jack Frost tapped the boulder with his
wand, and it closed around the wings

once more. Then it rolled back into its place.

Flying low, Rachel and Kirsty darted over to hide behind the magical boulder. They tried to prise it apart, but they couldn't even see where it was supposed to open. For a few moments, they could only think about getting the silver wings back. They were so close!

"Did you forget to watch out for me?" said Jack Frost in a hissing voice. "What

a mistake. How dare
you follow me here?
How dare you hitch
a ride on my cloud?"

He took a step
towards them, his
pointed beard quivering
in fury.

"I've got an
idea," said Kirsty
in Rachel's ear.
"We have to make him even angrier."

"Pardon?" said Rachel, feeling confused.

"Only his magic can open the boulder,"
said Kirsty. "We have to make him so
cross that he stamps his feet again."

She flew around behind Jack Frost,
making him turn to look at her. Now he
had his back to the magical boulder.

"You're not really very scary," she said.
"You're just a bit of a silly billy."

"What?" Jack Frost bellowed.

Rachel flew over to hover beside her
best friend.

"That's right," she said. "You're just
a great big softy really, aren't you?
Coochy-coochy-coo."

Jack Frost went purple with rage.

"No one has ever dared to say that to
me before!" he roared.

STAMP!

"Maybe we should start calling you
Frosty Fluff Pot," said Kirsty, her heart
thumping.

"Silence!" Jack Frost croaked.

STAMP!

"Or Jackie-pops?" Rachel suggested.

At this, Jack Frost became so angry that

he was unable to speak.

STAMP!

The boulder rolled up behind him, but he was too cross to notice. He raised his wand to cast a spell, and Rachel flew at him as fast as she could, knocking his wand arm against the boulder.

CRACK! The boulder opened to reveal the silver wings.

A Dream Come True

Kirsty whooshed forward and scooped the silver wings up in her arms. She hovered above the mountaintop and Rachel flew up to join her.

"Fools!" Jack Frost screeched. "There is no escape!"

He pointed his wand at them, and
began muttering a spell.

"Look!" Rachel cried.

Sianne was zooming towards them over
the snowy mountaintops. Before Jack

Frost could finish the words of his spell,
Sianne's magic had whisked Rachel and
Kirsty back to her home. Breathless and

delighted, they stood in the open doorway
of her glass home and handed her the
silver wings. Butterflies were already
fluttering around
the butterfly
bushes and all
the goblins had
disappeared.

"Everything is
back to normal,"
said Sianne,
smiling.

"In the human
world too?" Kirsty asked.

"Yes," said Sianne. "How can I ever
thank you enough?"

She put her arms around Rachel and
Kirsty, and they shared a tight hug.

"You don't need to thank us," said

Rachel, kissing Sianne's cheek. "It was our pleasure to be able to do something to help."

"I hope that you will come and visit me next time you come to Fairyland," said Sianne.

"We'd love to," Kirsty said.

"And remember," Sianne went on. "Butterflies carry messages for the fairies. From now on, whenever you see a butterfly in the human world, it will be a message from me, sending you my love."

"We will never forget," Rachel promised her friend.

Sianne raised her wand, and in a flurry of sparkles, the girls were back outside the hilltop glider station at the Butterfly Centre.

"Let's go and see if things are back to normal here as well," said Kirsty.

They stepped inside, and saw Meg smiling.

"I must have made a mistake," she was saying. "There's no sign of a rip."

"And all our equipment is in order," Harry added. "Ready to fly, Sunny?"

Everyone watched, smiling, as Sunny was lifted out of her wheelchair and into the glider at the crest of the hill. Harry strapped himself in beside her. Then Rachel and Kirsty held hands as the glider left the ground and lifted Sunny up into the blue sky. Harry flew the

glider in large, swooping circles around
the Butterfly Centre, before bringing it

back to the hilltop where everyone was
waiting. The glider landed with a slight
bump, and everyone cheered and clapped.

Sunny had the biggest smile that the girls had ever seen.

"Dreams really do come true," they heard her say.

When it was Rachel and Kirsty's turn, they decided to go up together – Rachel with Harry and Kirsty with Meg. They felt a tingle of excitement as the gliders left the hilltop, and then they were soaring up side by side. They looked across at each other and laughed.

"It's just like being fairies," Kirsty called out.

"Or butterflies!" Rachel called back. "Definitely the best feeling in the world!"

The End

Now it's time for Kirsty and Rachel to help...

Samira the Superhero Fairy

Read on for a sneak peek...

"I love absolutely everything about summer," said Kirsty Tate, who was skipping down Tippington High Street with her best friend Rachel Walker. "I love the sunshine and the long days – and most of all I love you staying with me for a whole week. We're going to have so much fun."

"I can't stop smiling," said Rachel. "I'm so excited about this film."

The girls were on their way to Tippington's little cinema. It was showing the brand-new summer blockbuster Dragon Girl and Tigerella, starring the girls' favourite superheroes.

"I can't wait to find out what adventures *Dragon Girl* and *Tigerella* are going to have," said Kirsty. "It's going to be amazing to see them in a film together – that's never happened before."

Read Samira the Superhero Fairy to find out what adventures are in store for Kirsty and Rachel!

Calling all parents, carers and teachers!
The Rainbow Magic fairies are here to help
your child enter the magical world of reading.
Whatever reading stage they are at, there's
a Rainbow Magic book for everyone!
Here is Lydia the Reading Fairy's guide to
supporting your child's journey at all levels.

Starting Out
Our Rainbow Magic Beginner Readers are perfect for first-time readers who are just beginning to develop reading skills and confidence. Approved by teachers, they contain a full range of educational levelling, as well as lively full-colour illustrations.

1

Developing Readers
Rainbow Magic Early Readers contain longer stories and wider vocabulary for building stamina and growing confidence. These are adaptations of our most popular Rainbow Magic stories, specially developed for younger readers in conjunction with an Early Years reading consultant, with full-colour illustrations.

2

Going Solo
The Rainbow Magic chapter books - a mixture of series and one-off specials - contain accessible writing to encourage your child to venture into reading independently. These highly collectible and much-loved magical stories inspire a love of reading to last a lifetime.

3

www.rainbowmagicbooks.co.uk

"Rainbow Magic got my daughter reading chapter books. Great sparkly covers, cute fairies and traditional stories full of magic that she found impossible to put down" - Mother of Edie (6 years)

"Florence LOVES the Rainbow Magic books. She really enjoys readi
- Mother of Florence (6 years)

The Rainbow Magic Reading Challenge

Well done, fairy friend – you have completed the book!
This book was worth 10 points.

See how far you have climbed on the
Reading Rainbow opposite.

The more books you read, the more points you will get,
and the closer you will be to becoming a Fairy Princess!

Do you want your own Reading Rainbow?
1. Cut out the coin below
2. Go to the Rainbow Magic website
3. Download and print out your poster
4. Add your coin and climb up the Reading Rainbow!

There's all this and lots more at
www.rainbowmagicbooks.co.uk

You'll find activities, competitions, stories, a special
newsletter and complete profiles of all the
Rainbow Magic fairies. Find a fairy with your name!